THE RED FOX MONSTER

For Liz

ISBN 0-439-27046-4

Copyright © 1996 by Alan Baron. All rights reserved. Published by Scholastic Inc., 555 Broadway, New York, NY 10012, by arrangement with Candlewick Press. SCHOLASTIC and associated logos are trademarks and/or registered trademarks of Scholastic Inc.

12 11 10 9 8 7 6 5 4 3 2 1   1 2 3 4 5 6/0

Printed in the U.S.A.   23

First Scholastic printing, March 2001

This book was typeset in Veronan.
The pictures were done in watercolor and ink.

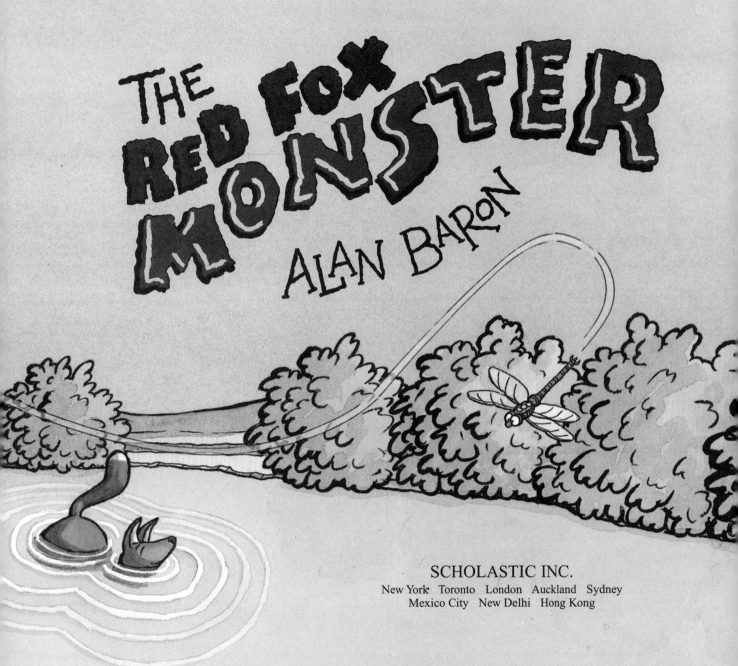

THE RED FOX MONSTER

ALAN BARON

SCHOLASTIC INC.

New York Toronto London Auckland Sydney
Mexico City New Delhi Hong Kong

Dan Dog and Tabby Cat were walking by the lake. On the bank they found Red Fox's clothes. "I have an idea," said Dan Dog.

They took Red Fox's clothes and put them on. Dan Dog rubbed dirt on his face then jumped onto Tabby Cat's shoulders. The Red Fox Monster hid behind a bush and waited.

Along came Little Pig.
Out jumped the Red Fox Monster
shouting, "DINNERTIME!"

"HELP, IT'S RED FOX!"
shouted Little Pig.
She turned and ran away.

Along came Lucy Goose, Big Duck, and Fat Hen. Out jumped the Red Fox Monster shouting, "DINNERTIME!"

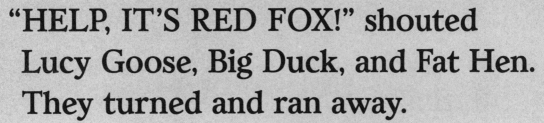

"HELP, IT'S RED FOX!" shouted
Lucy Goose, Big Duck, and Fat Hen.
They turned and ran away.

Along came Red Fox.
Out jumped the Red Fox Monster
shouting, "DINNERTIME!"

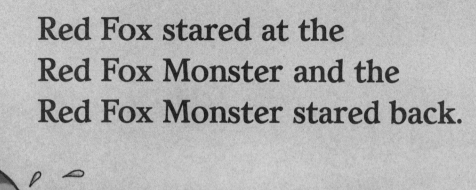

Red Fox stared at the
Red Fox Monster and the
Red Fox Monster stared back.

Then Red Fox gave a great big yell.
"HELP, IT'S RED FOX!"
And he turned and ran
and jumped back into the lake.

Red Fox swam away fast, then stopped.
"WAIT A MINUTE!" he shouted.
"YOU'RE NOT RED FOX, I'M RED FOX!"

Dan Dog and Tabby Cat
threw off Red Fox's clothes.
"Time to go!" said Dan Dog.
"Good idea!" said Tabby Cat.
And off they went.